A NOTE TO PARENTS

Reading Aloud with Your Child

Research shows that reading books aloud is the single most valuable support parents can provide in helping children learn to read.

- Be a ham! The more enthusiasm you display, the more your child will enjoy the book.
- Run your finger underneath the words as you read to signal that the print carries the story.
- Leave time for examining the illustrations more closely; encourage your child to find things in the pictures.
- Invite your youngster to join in whenever there's a repeated phrase in the text.
- Link up events in the book with similar events in your child's life.
- If your child asks a question, stop and answer it. The book can be a means to learning more about your child's thoughts.

Listening to Your Child Read Aloud

The support of your attention and praise is absolutely crucial to your child's continuing efforts to learn to read.

- If your child is learning to read and asks for a word, give it immediately so that the meaning of the story is not interrupted. DO NOT ask your child to sound out the word.
- On the other hand, if your child initiates the act of sounding out, don't intervene.
- If your child is reading along and makes what is called a miscue, listen for the sense of the miscue. If the word "road" is substituted for the word "street," for instance, no meaning is lost. Don't stop the reading for a correction.
- If the miscue makes no sense (for example, "horse" for "house"), ask your child to reread the sentence because you're not sure you understand what's just been read.
- Above all else, enjoy your child's growing command of print and make sure you give lots of praise. *You are your child's first teacher — and the most important one. Praise from you is critical for further risk-taking and learning.*

— Priscilla Lynch
Ph.D. New York University
Educational Consultant

To Gina Shaw,
who spells very well
— G.M.

To Samuel Gus Ziebel
and Jordan Emily Zwetchkenbaum
— B.L.

Text copyright © 1996 by Grace Maccarone.
Illustrations copyright © 1996 by Betsy Lewin.
All rights reserved. Published by Scholastic Inc.
HELLO READER!, CARTWHEEL BOOKS, and the CARTWHEEL BOOKS
logo are registered trademarks of Scholastic Inc.

Library of Congress Cataloging-in-Publication Data

Maccarone, Grace.
    Recess mess / by Grace Maccarone; illustrated by Betsy Lewin.
      p.   cm. — (First-grade friends) (Hello reader! Level 1)
    Summary: First-grade boys and girls go out to play at recess.
    ISBN 0-590-73878-X
    [1. Play — Fiction. 2. Schools — Fiction. 3. Stories in rhyme.]
    I. Lewin, Betsy, ill. II. Title. III. Series. IV. Series:
    Maccarone, Grace. First-grade friends.
  PZ8.3.M217Re   1996
[E] — dc20   95-36016
                                              CIP
                                              AC

12 11 10 9 8 7 6 5 4 3 2   6 7 8 9/9 0 1/0

Printed in the U.S.A.   23

First Scholastic printing, September 1996

Recess Mess

by Grace Maccarone
Illustrated by Betsy Lewin

Hello Reader! — Level 1

SCHOLASTIC INC.
New York Toronto London Auckland Sydney

Sam, Dan, Pam,
Kim, Max, and Jan
put away books
as fast as they can.

They put on coats.

They get in line.

They go outside.
It's recess time.

Dan runs.

Pam rolls.

Max slides.

Kim crawls.

Jan climbs.

Sam swings.

Sam swings.

Sam falls.

Dan throws. Pam catches.

Jan dances. Max hops.

Kim skips.

Sam jumps.

Sam jumps. Sam stops.

Sam looks for the boys' room.
He needs to go.
He sees two doors.
But wait! Oh, no!
Sam never used
this room before.
Sam tries to read
what's on the door.

B-O-Y?
G-I-R-L?
But Sam can't read.
And Sam can't spell.

What should Sam do?
Which should Sam use?
Sam gets an idea
to help him choose.

Sam will wait
and wait some more
for a boy or a girl
to come out of the door.

Now Sam is happy.
Sam feels swell.
He knows how to read
and he knows how to spell—

B-O-Y and G-I-R-L.